Super Pet-Sitter

written by Gina Bellisario

illustrated by Jessika von Innerebner

raintree

a Capstone company — publishers for children

CONTENTS

Raintree is an imprint of Capstone Global Library Limited, a company incorporated in England and Wales having its registered office at Meridian House, Sandy Lane West, Littlemore, Oxford, OX4 6LB – Registered company number: 6695582

www.raintree.co.uk
myorders@raintree.co.uk

Edited by Alison Deering
Designed by Lori Bye
Original illustrations © Stone Arch B
Illustrated by Jessika von Innerebner
Printed and bound in India

ISBN 978 1 4747 4949 7
22 21 20 19 18
10 9 8 7 6 5 4 3 2 1

British Library Cataloguing in Publication Data
A full catalogue record for this book is available from the British Library.

Every effort has been made to contact copyright holders of material reproduced in this book. Any omissions will be rectified in subsequent printings if notice is given to the publisher.

For Sofia, a mighty pup sitter – love, Mum

CHAPTER 1

Super hamster helper

It was just another day in the city of Winkopolis.
Duckies quacked. Toddlers babbled. Mummies cooed.
Everyone was doing the same old ordinary things.
Everyone, that is, but the girl who lived at 8 Louise
Lane.

That girl was Ellie Ultra. She was cleaning up
her classroom at Winkopolis Primary School, faster

than a falcon with rocket-powered wings. It was
*extra*ordinary.

Ellie raced across the floor like a roller coaster.
She picked up puzzle pieces and building blocks
during indoor break-time. Outside the window, rain
fell on the playground.

"Hamster coming through!" Ellie announced as
a fast-moving ball rolled behind her.

Running inside was Squeak, the class's new pet
hamster. Squeak had fuzzy hair and puffy cheeks
and twitchy whiskers. When he talked it sounded like,
"Squeak, squeak, squeak!"

Every day, one lucky pupil from Miss Little's class
got to be Squeak's official Hamster Helper. That
meant feeding him and giving him fresh water. It also
meant making sure he exercised.

Ellie had been waiting forever to be Hamster
Helper. Finally, it was her turn. It was different

than her usual superhero work. But it was still as important as catching bad guys. More than anything, she wanted to do a good job.

Ellie cleared the way as Squeak ran around in his ball. She swept up knights that had been left over from Joshua and Owen's chess game. She pushed aside sponge blocks, which Amelia and Amanda were using to build a scale model of the town's shopping centre.

On the class comfy chair, Ellie's best friend, Hannah, was reading a comic book from her favourite series, Dance Cat Academy. The hamster raced happily towards her. "Squeak, squeak!"

Ellie quickly flexed her muscle power. She lifted the chair - with Hannah still in it - over her head.

"Cuckoo bananas, Ellie!" Hannah cried. She looked down as the ball rolled right under her.

"Maybe next time, Squeak could go *around* the chair?"

Ellie carefully lowered her friend to the ground. "Sorry, Hannah," she replied. "But it's my job to look after Squeak. That means I need to stop him from running into things, like chairs or children. Or chairs with children in them."

At last, the ball rolled to a stop in the corner of the room.

"Whew!" Ellie sighed. "Taking care of Squeak is tiring. Even more tiring than battling a super-villain!" She bent over to pick up the ball and accidentally bumped the desk behind her.

"Hey! Watch out!" a voice snapped.

Ellie turned and saw Dex Diggs, the official class villain. Dex wasn't a *real* villain. At least not like the smelly, spiky, snorty ones Ellie usually faced. But he was never up to any good.

Sure enough, Dex stuck out his tongue. Then he opened his maths folder and took out an old worksheet. He folded the paper in half, expertly creasing it.

"What are you making?" Ellie asked.

"Duh!" Dex's eyes rolled towards the ceiling. "It's a paper aeroplane."

"Miss Little said paper aeroplanes aren't allowed in the classroom," Ellie said "She doesn't want anything flying around. Well, except superheroes."

"I'm going to fly it after school," Dex replied. "If you're in the sky, you should probably watch out." He aimed the aeroplane in Ellie's direction and smiled wickedly.

Ellie held Squeak's ball closely. "Don't worry, I'll keep you safe from that troublemaker," she whispered to the hamster.

Just then their teacher, Miss Little, jingled her wind chime. Break was over. While everyone cleaned up,

Ellie walked over to Squeak's cage. She opened the ball and let him crawl inside, then sat down with the rest of the class.

"Girls and boys, I have a very special announcement," Miss Little said. "It's about our pet hamster."

The class leaned forward eagerly.

"You have all been great Hamster Helpers during the school day," the teacher said. "But, as it turns out, I need someone to look after Squeak this weekend. I won't be able to bring him home like usual." She smiled. "Do I have any volunteers?"

Hands shot up around the room.

"I'll take care of Squeak!" Amanda offered.

"Pick me!" said Owen. "I can show Squeak my new collection of bow ties. I have a striped bow tie and a bow tie that plays music. There's even one that lights up!"

As more children volunteered, Ellie sat quietly. Squeak was small, but watching him for two whole days would be a big job. She didn't want to make any mistakes.

Still, Miss Little needed someone to save her. And Ellie was a superhero, after all! After a moment, her hand went up with the rest.

"Wow, it looks like everyone wants to help," Miss Little said. "To be fair, I'll draw a name from our class jar." She took out the jar, which contained the names of all her pupils, and shook it around. Then she pulled out a name. "Ellie Ultra."

"Ellie?" Dex's face soured. "She won't be any good at caring for Squeak."

"I'll take good care of Squeak," Ellie promised, ignoring the villain. "I'll feed him and give him fresh water. And I'll protect him from space invaders."

"I'm sure you will," Miss Little said with a wink. "But first, ask your parents for their permission. If they're OK with it, you can bring Squeak home on Friday." She patted Squeak's cage. "Thank you for taking on the job."

"Super Hamster Helper, at your service!" Ellie said.

CHAPTER 2

Shrinker clinker

Ellie raced out of the door as soon as school ended. She couldn't wait to ask her parents about hamster sitting over the weekend. She also couldn't wait to get away from Dex and his pesky paper plane.

At home, Ellie threw her rucksack on the kitchen chair. "Mum and Dad, your hero is here!" she called.

Four happy feet ran up to her. "Ruff, ruff!" Super Fluffy, Ellie's stuffed-animal-turned-real-life dog, barked a greeting. A toy dangled from his mouth.

"What are you playing with, Fluffster?" Ellie looked closer at the toy, and her jaw dropped. "Hey, give that back. It's my Elasticband Dude action figure!"

She pulled at the doll, but Super Fluffy pulled back. Soon they were caught up in a superhero tug of war. Elasticband Dude stretched like chewing gum until - *SNAP!* - the doll snapped in half.

Super Fluffy dropped his half and retreated through the doorway of Mum and Dad's laboratory.

"Poor Elasticband Dude," Ellie said, picking up the broken piece. "You're no match for Super Fluffy. Or should I say, Destructo Dog?" She placed the pieces next to her rucksack, then followed her pup downstairs.

Super Fluffy ran ahead of Ellie as she flew into the lab. It was an extraordinary place. There was a library with books about stardust and a fridge full of fruit, vegetables and fungi. A long worktop stretched down the middle of the room. It held rows of colourful liquids in containers. On a large whiteboard, numbers and letters had been written down. Then, after a second thought, they'd been scribbled out.

Then there were Mum and Dad's inventions. Like art in a museum, they were on display in the Gadget Gallery. There was the Ultra Magnifier, which could show the freckles on a flea. There was the Ultra Echo-Echo-Echo, which could make a sound travel for miles.

Ellie's parents were super-genius scientists who used their intelligence for good. They had built the

inventions for B.R.A.I.N., a group that caught evil-doers.

It took brainpower to make a gadget, but it also took noise - lots and lots of noise. In the lab, there was always something dripping, honking or exploding. Today was noisier than usual. Beakers bubbled. Formulas fizzed.

Suddenly, from the far end of the room, there came a . . . *C-C-C-CLINK!*

Uh-oh. That doesn't sound good, Ellie thought. She flew past the Gadget Gallery and peeked around the corner.

In the lab's testing station, two new inventions lay flat on the ground. They were round like Squeak's hamster wheel but big enough to fit on Ellie's bike. Spokes connected to a large platform in the middle.

One of the inventions was flickering oddly. Ellie's parents were staring hard at it through the visors of their Ultra Safety Suits, which they wore whenever they were testing a gadget. They looked confused. Their heads popped up as Ellie skipped into the station.

"I heard something strange," Ellie said. "It sounded a bit like a tap-dancing robo-beast."

"Unfortunately, it was the Ultra Shrinker," Mum said, pointing to the flickering gadget. "It's not working as well as the Ultra Grower." She nodded to the gadget that sat next to the shrinker.

"There must be a bug in it," Dad added, scratching his head.

Blinking on her X-ray vision, Ellie scanned the Ultra Shrinker. She searched for creepy-crawly insects, but her eye beams only revealed a pile of microchips.

"I can't see any bugs," she said. "No stinkbugs, bedbugs, June bugs -"

Dad chuckled. "A *computer* bug, I mean. It's a virus that infects a computer. It must've made one of the microchips sick."

"Maybe you could give it some chicken soup?" Ellie suggested. She cracked herself up.

"If only it were that easy," Dad said. "But there are one hundred and eleven microchips in there. It's hard to tell which one is sick. The Ultra Shrinker is supposed to shrink objects, but sometimes it just makes an awful clinking noise."

"Can you show me?" Ellie asked.

"Of course." Mum opened the glass door of the station and disappeared. She came back with a cherry from the laboratory fridge and popped it on the Ultra Grower's platform.

A moment later, the gadget flashed like a camera. Suddenly, the cherry got bigger . . . and bigger . . . and bigger . . .

When the cherry finally stopped growing, it was as big as a beach ball.

"Cuckoo bananas!" Ellie cried. "You'd need a super-size appetite to eat that!"

"Now we can try the Ultra Shrinker." Mum picked up the cherry and placed it on the shrinker.

Seconds passed, but nothing happened. Super Fluffy sniffed the invention, when suddenly, there came a . . . *C-C-C-CLINK!*

"Yikes! That *does* sound awful," Ellie said.

Mum nodded. "That's not the worst part. Both of these inventions are due at B.R.A.I.N. headquarters by Monday. That's one week away! It will be tough to fix the shrinker in time." She let out a noisy sigh. "We have a big job ahead of us."

A big job! Ellie thought. That reminded her to ask about hamster sitting.

"Mum? Dad?" she began. "Miss Little needs someone to look after our class hamster this weekend, and I was picked. Can I?" Ellie clasped her hands together. "Pretty please . . . with a humongous cherry on top?"

Ellie's parents exchanged worried looks.

"I'm not sure, sweetie," Mum said. "If you're taking care of the hamster, then who will look after Super Fluffy?"

"Ruff, ruff!" Over by the Gadget Gallery, Super Fluffy barked excitedly at a large lizard tank.

Inside the tank was Cyclops, the Ultras' giant, one-eyed iguana. Cyclops was busy enjoying his new hobby - crocheting. He had crocheted slippers, a hat, a stuffed owl and a tail warmer. He was now finishing a Christmas jumper.

A strand of wool dangled close to the ground. With his tail wagging, Super Fluffy snapped up the strand. He took off running across the lab. Cyclops's eye popped open as his crocheted creation began to unravel.

Lightning-quick, Ellie bolted ahead of Super Fluffy. After turning invisible, she jumped into his path. Super Fluffy ran straight into her arms.

"Rrrr?" The pup watched curiously as the string seemed to free itself from his mouth.

Holding the string, Ellie reappeared. "I've stopped you now, Destructo Dog."

Ellie gathered the rest of the unravelled wool while Super Fluffy whimpered behind her. "I'm sorry, Cy," she said, returning a mess of red and green to the lizard's tank. "Super Fluffy only wanted to play. He didn't mean to ruin your jumper."

Cyclops hissed at Ellie's pup. Then he started a new Christmas jumper.

"Yesterday, Super Fluffy played in the flower bed," Mum said. "He dug up the gladioli."

"And the day before that, he was fetching his ball in the lab," Dad added. "He spilled animal-print formula on one of my lab coats. Now the coat looks like a spotted hyena!"

He sighed at the coat, then turned back to Ellie. "Super Fluffy needs your attention, or else he can get into mischief. It will be hard to look after him with another pet around."

"I'll keep Super Fluffy out of trouble," Ellie told her parents. "He's easier to stop than a sludge monster, and I took care of that last week."

"I suppose so . . ." Dad said.

"Besides, he'll be on his best behaviour for our guest." Ellie raised her eyebrow at Super Fluffy. "You'll behave for Squeak. Won't you, Fluffster?"

Super Fluffy looked up innocently.

"Well . . ." Mum made a face. It was the same face she made when a formula was about to go *KA-BOOM!* "OK," she said at last. "But we're counting on you to take care of everything."

Ellie poked the sky with her finger. "Have no fear. The mighty pet sitter is here!"

CHAPTER 3

A hairy scare

The days flew by in a flash. When school ended on Friday, it was finally time: Ellie would be Squeak's Hamster Helper for the weekend!

Miss Little helped Ellie get ready. She got a bag of bedding and a chew stick for Squeak from the classroom supplies.

"Make sure you change Squeak's bedding," Miss Little said. "And keep the chew stick in his cage. A hamster's teeth are always growing, so they need something to chew. That stops their teeth getting too long." She put the supplies in a small tote bag. "Now we need Squeak's food."

Ellie grabbed a bag of seed mix from her teacher's desk. "Squeak gets one scoop every day. Right?"

"That's right," Miss Little replied. "For a treat, you can give him a piece of sweet potato. Fruit is also OK for hamsters to eat."

Ellie counted out the instructions on her fingers, trying to keep track of what Miss Little said. She didn't want to forget her hamster duties, but it was hard remembering them all.

1. *Change Squeak's bedding.*

2. *Give him a chew stick.*

3. *Put one scoop of food in his bowl.*

"Which treat is OK again?" Ellie asked. "I suppose my memory isn't so super."

"No need to memorize everything. I wrote the instructions down for you." Miss Little handed over a note card. It read:

Hamster helper duties for the weekend:

1. *In the morning, give one scoop of seed mix.*

2. *In the afternoon, give one small treat.**

3. *Keep water bottle filled.*

4. *Change bedding once - should be 3-5 centimetres deep in the cage.*

a treat = a small piece of sweet potato or fruit

"Cherries seem to be Squeak's favourite fruit," Miss Little said. "You can give him one if you have any."

Ellie giggled to herself. Thanks to the Ultra Grower, she had a cherry that could feed Squeak for an entire year!

When Ellie and Miss Little had packed up the rest of the supplies, it was time to get Squeak. A small worry struck Ellie's stomach. It grew as she thought about her hamster duties ahead. Finally, it was too big to hold inside.

"Miss Little, I'm a bit worried about looking after Squeak," Ellie said quietly.

Her teacher paused. "Oh?"

Ellie nodded. "I want to do a good job," she said. "But I've only ever looked after him for one day. What if I make a mistake? I could forget to give him fresh water. Or, I don't know, I could let an evil sorcerer turn him into an ogre."

"It's OK to be nervous when doing something new," Miss Little replied. She gave Ellie an encouraging smile. "Just try your best, and you'll do brilliantly."

* * *

Ellie usually flew home from school, but all week long, Dex had been launching his paper plane at her. It always missed, but Ellie didn't want to deal with another annoying air attack. So today, Mum drove Ellie and Squeak home.

In the car, Ellie held the cage on her lap. "I'll try my best to take care of you," she told Squeak.

"Squeak, squeak!" the hamster replied.

When they walked in the front door, Ellie lifted the cage so that Squeak could have a look around. "This is your home for the weekend," she told him. "I hope you like it."

Mum put the bag of supplies on a chair and peeked at Squeak. The hamster was busy nestling in his bedding.

"He's getting settled in already," she said.

"That's my mum," Ellie told Squeak. "She's a scientist - but *not* a mad scientist, so you don't have to worry. She only gets mad when I don't tidy my room."

In the kitchen, Dad was sitting with his *A Is for Atom* magazine and drinking a coffee. Ellie placed the cage on the table in front of him.

"And here's my dad," she said to the hamster.

Dad lowered his mug. "My, what a cute omnivore!" he said as Squeak ate some of his hamster food.

Ellie's eyebrows squeezed together in confusion. "Omni-what?"

"*Omnivore.* It's an animal that eats plants and other animals," Dad explained. "Hamsters eat food that comes from plants. But they also snack on certain kinds of insects."

Ellie bent down to Squeak. "Dad is a scientist too," she whispered. "He talks like one every now and then. You'll get used to it."

Just then, Super Fluffy charged in with his toy football. He was eager to play fetch. Like a furry comet, he flew through the kitchen and jumped on Ellie, catching her by surprise.

"Whoa, Fluffster!" Ellie cried. She flew backwards and bumped into Dad's mug.

Coffee sprayed in every direction. In a blink, Ellie grabbed the mug and zigzagged across the floor, catching every last tiny drop.

As Ellie returned the mug to Dad, Super Fluffy caught sight of Squeak. His tail started wagging. He had found a new friend to play with!

Ellie held Super Fluffy up to the cage. "And *this* is Super Fluffy," she said to Squeak. "He's a dog. But sometimes, he acts like a robo-beast that's gone bonkers."

Super Fluffy poked his nose at Squeak and sniffed.

"Squeak, squeak!" The hamster scurried away, escaping into his hideaway hut.

Squeak is scared of Super Fluffy, Ellie realized. To the hamster, Super Fluffy probably looked like a giant drooling hairball.

"Squeak isn't used to dogs," Ellie told her pup. She put him back on the ground. "Better give him space so you don't scare him."

Ellie took Squeak's cage into the living room and placed it on top of a tall chest. The chest was near a bright window but out of direct sunlight, just like Miss Little had suggested. It was the perfect place to keep Squeak.

After taping her teacher's instructions to the cage, Ellie tried to make the hamster feel at home. She read him *The Bewitching Ball*, the newest Princess Power comic book. At dinner, she shared some of her sweet potato. She also stopped Super

Fluffy from running off with her dessert.

At bedtime, Ellie brought a lamp into the living room and plugged it in next to the cage.

"In case you're scared of the dark, this will help," she told Squeak. She turned off the other lights, then headed upstairs to bed. "Good night, Squeak! Sweet potato dreams!"

Ellie went down the corridor to her room. But before she reached the door, her supersonic hearing picked up a familiar noise.

"Squeak, squeak!"

That's Squeak! He might be in trouble! Ellie thought. She hurried back to the living room and gasped.

On the wall, an enormous shadow puppet loomed over the cage. It changed shape in the glow of the lamp. First it was a bear, then a unicorn, then a turkey on a tricycle.

It had to be the work of the Shadow Puppet Master. That villain was an expert at using shadow puppets to do his dirty deeds. Lately, his puppets had been showing up in Mum and Dad's laboratory. He always sent them to steal her parents' powerful gadgets.

Ellie knew there was only one way to get rid of the shadowy minions. Turn off the light!

"It's lights out for you, pesky puppets!" Ellie shouted.

She reached behind the cage to turn off the lamp when she saw Squeak in the light. He was running on his hamster wheel and casting shadow puppets on the wall!

Ellie suddenly remembered what Miss Little had said during science. Hamsters were nocturnal animals. That meant they were most active at night.

Ellie laughed at her mistake. "I thought you were a villain," she said to Squeak. "But you're only guilty of staying up past bedtime."

With a yawn, Ellie headed to bed. Her first full day of Squeak-sitting awaited her in the morning!

CHAPTER 4

Hide-and-squeak

"Look! Squeak is peeking out of his tunnel," Hannah said on Saturday. She pointed at the hamster cage. "He's playing peekaboo. Or should I say, *Squeak-aboo?*"

Ellie's best friend had come over to help change the hamster's bedding. Hannah had assisted Miss Little with the job last week. Because Ellie wanted to make sure she did it just right, she had called her super bestie for help.

As Ellie moved the cage to the floor, Hannah opened a new bag of bedding. Ellie placed Squeak in a plastic tub so she could clean out the old shavings. Hannah added some toys and a chew stick to keep him entertained.

After throwing away the used bedding, the girls put down a new layer. Squeak watched from the tub while nibbling his chew stick. When they had finished, Ellie scooped up the hamster.

"Easy there, little wiggler," she said as he squirmed in her hands. "You're hard to hold on to, you know that?"

Quickly, she placed him back inside the cage. Then she went to the kitchen with Hannah to wash up.

"Squeak is *so* cute," Hannah said. "I wish I could have been Hamster Helper for the weekend. How's it going?"

"I've been as busy as a beaver android!" Ellie replied. "This morning, I gave him breakfast and read him the rest of my Princess Power comic books. He squeaked while I read. It must be his favourite series."

"Oh, that reminds me!" Hannah bounce-clapped. "I have news about Dance Cat Academy!"

Just then, a string of high-pitched squeaking noises came from the living room. The girls shared surprised glances and raced around the corner.

Super Fluffy was crouching on the floor, peeking into the hamster cage.

Oh no! I forgot to put the cage back on the chest! Ellie thought. She watched as Super Fluffy pawed at the door for Squeak to come out and play. The hamster squeaked from inside his hideaway hut.

"Stop, Super Fluffy!" she said firmly. "Go and find something else to play with."

At Ellie's voice, Super Fluffy jumped. He knocked over a table, spilling a vase of lilies before scrambling out of sight.

Ellie sighed at the lilies, which were now lying in a puddle of water. She placed her hands on the

puddle and steamed the water away using her super-heating power. After refilling the vase, she returned the flowers to their original spot.

"I guess Super Fluffy is keeping you busy too," Hannah said.

"He can be a handful, that's for sure," Ellie replied. "This morning he stuck his nose right in Dad's mixture for tie-dyed food colouring. He looked like an Easter egg until I washed the mixture off him."

"Take a break tomorrow," Hannah said. "It's Dance Day at Winkopolis Books & Toys. That's what I was going to tell you!"

Winkopolis Books & Toys hosted lots of special events. There was Beach Party Day and Talk-Like-a-Spy Day. Ellie especially loved Comic Book Day. It was the best ever.

"Really?" Ellie asked excitedly.

Hannah nodded. "There's going to be a trivia game about Dance Cat Academy. First prize is a poster of all the characters - Fifi, Ginger, Clawdine . . . and KitKat!" She jingled her bracelet, which had charms of KitKat, her most-beloved character from the comic book series. "Let's go!"

"Yeah! That'd be great -" Ellie started to say, when suddenly, Super Fluffy ran past with her slipper. He had found something to play with, just as Ellie had told him to do. It just wasn't exactly what she'd had in mind.

Ellie's face fell. As much as she wanted to go to Dance Day, she needed to keep an eye on Super Fluffy, especially with Squeak around. It looked like she would have to miss out on the fun with her friend.

"On second thoughts, I'd better skip Dance Day," she told Hannah. "I have to be on pup patrol tomorrow. I promised my parents I'd watch Super Fluffy. And Squeak, of course. It's my last day to take care of him."

"OK. Well, I better get home for lunch."

After Hannah left, Ellie put the cage back on top of the chest - safely out of Super Fluffy's reach. If she was going to be a mighty pet sitter, she couldn't make any more mistakes.

"It's time for Squeak's afternoon treat," she said, scanning Miss Little's instructions. She remembered the cherries in the laboratory fridge and zipped downstairs. "One cherry, coming up!"

Poking around the fridge, Ellie found a red, ripe cherry behind a bowl of mushrooms. She closed the door and heard a *C-C-C-CLINK!* It was the Ultra Shrinker!

The gadget sat on the work table, surrounded by Mum and Dad's tinkering tools. It was flickering as oddly as before. Mum and Dad shook their heads at the invention, then at each other.

Ellie flew over. "I heard the shrinker thingy. Is it still broken?"

"I'm afraid so," Mum said. "We tried getting rid of the gadget's computer virus. We ran tests, made observations . . . Dad even sang 'Twinkle, Twinkle, Little Gadget.'"

At that, Dad threw his hands up and smiled weakly.

"It won't do much good for B.R.A.I.N. if it only works some of the time," Mum continued. She picked up the Ultra Shrinker and walked over to the Gadget Gallery. There, she dropped it into a bin of leftover parts, which were recycled into new gadgets. "We need to build another one."

"You're making a whole new Ultra Shrinker?" Ellie asked.

Dad grabbed a blueprint from the shelf. "A super-genius scientist's work is never done!" He unrolled the blueprint across the work table, then started reading it over with Mum.

Ellie left her parents to their work and headed upstairs to bring Squeak his cherry. A Hamster Helper's work was never done either!

* * *

When bedtime rolled around, Ellie turned on the lamp behind the cage. A shadow of a witch on a broomstick appeared on the wall. It looked like the wicked work of the Shadow Puppet Master, but it was only Squeak. He was running on his wheel in the lamplight.

"You're as busy as a beaver android too. Aren't you, Squeak?" she asked.

"Squeak, squeak!" the hamster happily replied.

Just then, Super Fluffy bounced over and dropped Ellie's slipper at her feet. The slipper was wet and slimy. He had attacked it with his super bad drool power.

Ellie's nose wrinkled as she picked up the slobbery slipper. "I see you've been busy having fun, Fluffster. But playtime is over for today."

She picked up the pup and went to get some rest. She had one more day to take care of Squeak, and she was determined to do a mighty job. Even with Destructo Dog on the loose!

CHAPTER 5

Destructo Dog strikes!

"Rise and squeak!" Ellie greeted the hamster as the sun came up on Sunday. In the living room, she took the cage down from the chest. Carefully, she placed it on the floor, then grabbed the bag of seed mix. "Ready for breakfast, little omnivore?"

Squeak scurried to his food bowl, and Ellie added a scoopful of seeds. Then she sat next to the cage and kept him company while he ate.

Mum walked in with her lab coat. "Good morning, Hamster Helper," she said. "You know, you've been taking great care of Squeak. Miss Little would be proud of you."

"Do you think so?" Ellie asked. "I'm trying my best to do a good job."

"Squeak is in *super* hands," Mum said. She glanced at the clock. "I better start building that new Ultra Shrinker with Dad. It's due at B.R.A.I.N. headquarters tomorrow. If you need anything, we'll be in the laboratory." She disappeared downstairs.

Ellie turned back to Squeak. "It's my last day of hamster duty. I promise to keep up the good work. I'll stop anything that stands in my way - even an army of zombie slugs!" She jumped up. "First, I need to get dressed."

Like an arrow, Ellie shot to her room and X-rayed her wardrobe. Her eye beams located her shirt, tights and skirt. But where was her cape? She looked around and spotted the crumpled cloth on Super Fluffy's bed.

"Super Fluffy must've used my cape for a blanket," she said, shaking off dog hair.

Just then, happy yapping filled the air. It sounded like Super Fluffy was having a puppy play date. But who could he be playing with?

"Squeak!" Ellie realized. She had forgotten to move the cage out of her pup's reach!

Ellie swooped into the living room. On the floor, Super Fluffy was crouched in front of the cage. He barked excitedly at the hamster and pawed at the door.

Suddenly the cage popped open, and Squeak raced out in a furry blur. As he ran across the room, Super Fluffy took off after him.

"Ruff, ruff!" the pup barked, his tail wagging wildly. He chased Squeak around a chair and under the curtains. He bounced on cushions and leaped over stools. Pillows flew. Furniture toppled. Super Fluffy plowed a path of canine destruction.

"Fluffster! Bad dog! Stop!" Ellie shouted. She darted left and right, rescuing tipped-over knick-knacks. Squeak scurried into the kitchen. Ellie flew after the hamster to pick him up when he disappeared under a storage trolley. With a terrific leap, Super Fluffy pounced on the trolley. As he jumped down, his hind legs kicked over a stack of bowls.

The bowls fell like a porcelain waterfall. Arms out, Ellie dove for them like a volley ball player diving for the ball. They landed in her hands.

"Phew!" Ellie cried with relief.

As she placed the bowls back on the trolley, Squeak ran out the other side. He headed towards Mum and Dad's laboratory and vanished through the doorway. Super Fluffy hurried after him.

"The lab is no place for a hamster - or Destructo Dog!" Ellie cried. She followed them down the stairs.

In the lab, Squeak scurried to the bin of leftover parts. It was overflowing with a mountain of mechanical stuff, including the broken Ultra Shrinker. The gadget was still flickering.

As Squeak ducked behind the bin, Super Fluffy bounded up. He bumped the bin and knocked the Ultra Shrinker to the floor.

Thunk!

"Squeak! Super Fluffy! Come here!" Ellie called. Racing past the bin, she stepped on the gadget's platform.

Just then the shrinker flashed.

Suddenly the lab started to grow. The ceiling got higher. The bookshelf got taller. Even the floor seemed to stretch until it was as wide as an ocean.

Moments later, the island in the middle of the lab towered over Ellie.

Ellie caught a glimpse of her reflection in the refrigerator door. She was no taller than a hamster! Next to her, the Ultra Shrinker, no longer flickering, looked like a human-sized hamster wheel.

The fall must've fixed whatever was broken on the Ultra Shrinker! Ellie realized. *Which means it was working when I stepped on it.*

That explained why the lab seemed so different. It hadn't got bigger - Ellie had gotten smaller.

Her eyes grew until they felt like they had doubled in size. "I've shrunk!"

CHAPTER 6

Hush little Ellie

Ellie looked frantically around the lab. She needed to get back to being a full-sized superhero again. And to do that, she needed the Ultra Grower!

Now where is that gadget? Ellie wondered. If anyone would know, it was two super geniuses called Mum and Dad.

"Muuum! Daaad!" Ellie called as instruments beeped and crackled. But the Ultra Shrinker had shrunk her vocal chords, making her voice much quieter. The noise from the lab easily swallowed it up.

"MUUUM! DAAAD!" Ellie called again, mustering the might of her little lungs. But it was no use. Her parents couldn't hear her.

If only they had Super Fluffy's ears, Ellie thought. *That dog can hear a chicken bone hitting the floor from anywhere.*

Just then the sound of a barking dog struck like thunder. *RUFF, RUFF!*

Ellie turned and came face-to-face with a giant, drooling hairball. She braced herself as Super Fluffy stuck out his long pink tongue and gave her the biggest, slobbery-est kiss ever.

"Super Fluffy!" Ellie hugged his leg. "I'm so glad to see you! I need you to call Mum and Dad. If you bark, they'll come running!"

Her furry friend seemed to understand. "Ruff, ruff! Ruff, ruff! Ruff, ruff!" Super Fluffy barked and barked.

Ellie plugged her ears as his voice boomed across the room. He was noisier than the lab's erupting volcano plants.

Dad came around the island. "Hmm, it looks like we have a visitor," he said, noticing Super Fluffy. He shook his head and walked over.

"Dad! It's me!" Ellie darted after Dad as he strolled past. Suddenly he stopped, and she bounced off of him, landing back on the ground.

Dad turned, a curious look on his face. He shrugged his shoulders and whisked up the pup. "Sorry, boy. No dogs allowed in the lab," he said. "We don't want your nose turning into a tie-dyed Easter egg again, now do we?"

He took Super Fluffy upstairs to the kitchen. As the pup whined, Dad closed the door before returning to the laboratory to work. Ellie was still trying to get on her feet again and fly after him when she saw Squeak crawling out from behind a cabinet.

It's my job to take care of Squeak, she thought. *I can't leave him by himself, even to find Mum and Dad. What if he gets lost? He could end up in the batch of wolf DNA!*

She doubted Miss Little would like a class pet that howled at the moon.

Ellie followed Squeak to the Gadget Gallery. He scurried up a ladder, then plopped into a pipe that was connected to the Ultra Hush-a-Bye. The gadget looked like an ordinary pipe organ, but it played the sweetest lullaby Ellie had ever heard. It was good at stopping evil-doers like Big Baby. If that villain didn't have a nap, well, look out.

The gadget's pipes played a sing-song melody. Suddenly - *Pop!* - Squeak popped out of a pipe with one of the notes. His tiny feet soared above the pipe before he dropped back inside another pipe when the note stopped.

Pop! Drop. *Pop!* Drop. Squeak flew up and down with the music like a ballerina with whiskers.

"Hopping hamsters!" Ellie cried. She went to catch him, but he popped out of the pipe behind her. She turned and tried again on the next note, but he popped out of a pipe at the end of the row. It was impossible to know where he'd come out next.

Unless . . . With a blink, Ellie scanned the inside of the Ultra Hush-a-Bye. Her X-ray beams revealed pipes that were labelled with a note from the musical alphabet. They poked out of a tunnel where Squeak was crawling. When a new note played, air blew through the tunnel and sent him up the pipe that was marked with a *C*.

Ellie breezed to the top, and out popped the hamster. "OOF!" she said, catching the big fuzzy ball. She sagged a little under Squeak's weight. "I guess you're heavier now that I'm your size," she said. "Either that, or you've had too many treats."

She turned away from the invention when Squeak started to squirm. His feet wiggled. His body jiggled. "I should call you Mr Wiggles!" she said, her grip slipping.

As Ellie struggled to hold on to Squeak, she flew closer to a weather vane invention that was spinning in the Gadget Gallery. She didn't notice the invention spinning towards her when - *THUMP!* - it bumped her from behind.

Ellie was thrown head first. Squeak flew out of her arms. Ellie turned like a windmill over Mum's extra jars of anti-stain formula before landing in a puddle on the storage counter.

"What a mucky mess!" She stuck out her tongue at the ooey-gooey liquid that surrounded her. It oozed from a bottle that was lying nearby.

"Extra-Strength Superglue," Ellie said, reading the label. She tried to shake off the glue. But it held her as strongly as a mutant spider's web.

Just then, excited squeaking noises came from Cyclops's tank. It was Squeak! He crawled into some dandelions that were piled high in the lizard's food dish. Hamsters loved eating dandelions as much as giant, one-eyed iguanas did.

Squeak munched on a dandelion, unaware that the iguana was also snacking. Cyclops was watching TV, mindlessly grabbing the leafy greens before throwing them down his baggy throat. He didn't see the hamster. His eye was glued to the latest episode of *Name That Reptile!*

Ellie gasped. She had to save Squeak from the iguana's snack attack. Or else, he was going to end up in the belly of a scaly beast!

CHAPTER 7

Bite-sized

Cyclops stared blankly at the TV as he reached for more dandelions. He was about to turn poor Squeak into lizard food, and he hadn't the foggiest idea.

"Cyclops might be the world's smartest reptile," Ellie said, "but when the TV is on, he has the IQ of a kidney bean."

The thick, sticky band of glue held Ellie in its clutches. She tried pulling herself out of the glue puddle, but she barely moved at all. Squeak had to be rescued before it was too late!

"C'mon, muscle power! Don't fail me now!" Ellie cried, lunging forward with all the strength she could muster. Her legs wobbled. Her arms shook. Tiny beads of sweat gathered on her equally tiny forehead.

The glue slowly stretched to the limits of gooey stretchiness when her sneaker slipped out from under her. Suddenly - *THWAP!* - she flew back into the puddle like a slingshot.

"Bluck!" Ellie made a yuck face, covered in even more glue. "There has to be a way to get free." Too bad Mum's anti-stick formula was in her desk at school. It came in handy whenever she had to unstick herself from Dex's chewing gum sculptures, which he usually left on the floor.

The glue bottle was lying next to her, its contents still leaking out. Ellie saw some large lettering on the bottle that read *WARNING: WILL MELT IN HEAT.*

"Heat?" She smiled and rubbed her hands together. "It's about to get hot in here!"

After sinking her hands into the puddle, Ellie activated her heating power. Her hands started glowing, growing hotter and hotter by the second. Soon bubbles formed on the surface as the glue rose to a blistering temperature.

"Melt, glue, melt!" Ellie cried.

She looked frantically between the glue and Cyclops's dish, where only a few dandelions - and Squeak - remained. The iguana went to grab the last handful when the glue around Ellie's fingers became thin and watery. In no time, the whole puddle lost its stickiness.

Whoosh! Ellie flew to her freedom. Like a shooting star, she soared straight to the iguana's tank and landed next to Squeak.

Ellie picked up a dandelion and shook it in front of Squeak. "Here, Squeaky-Squeak!" she coaxed. "Come and get it!"

"Squeak, squeak!" The hamster eagerly followed Ellie away from the dish just as Cyclops grabbed the rest of the flowers. She led Squeak past the iguana's crochet hook and stuffed owl.

A newly crocheted Christmas jumper was hanging over the tank. Ellie ran up the jumper with Squeak climbing behind her. When they reached the top, she hoisted him into her arms and took off.

They hadn't travelled far before Squeak started wiggling again. Ellie fought to keep her grip, but it was impossible to keep holding him. She needed a spot to land - fast.

A desk appeared up ahead. Ellie floated over and plopped him next to a large, rolled-up blueprint.

"Whew!" she said with a sigh. "Squeak, you are as squirmy as a radioactive worm."

In the distance, Mum and Dad were building a new Ultra Shrinker at their work table. A round invention was leaning up against Dad's stool.

"The Ultra Grower!" Ellie said.

Ellie needed to get over there, but she couldn't leave Squeak behind to fly to the grower. He was so fast he'd disappear in an instant. And there was no telling what kind of trouble he'd get into in the lab.

But maybe her parents could help . . . *if* she could get their attention. Ellie ran to a cup holder and grabbed sparkly pom-poms off the ends of two pencils.

"Mum! Dad! Over here!" she cried, shaking the pom-poms overhead. "I'm the smallest superhero

ever . . . well, if you don't count Astro Ant from my comic book!"

Mum was twisting wires. Dad was drilling holes. It was as if they were in their own little tool-tinkering world. Ellie remembered they needed to finish the gadget for B.R.A.I.N. The chances of them looking up were slim.

Ellie lowered the pom-poms. Nothing could keep a scientist's attention like a good, old-fashioned problem.

"I have my own problem to worry about. Don't I, Squeak?" she said, trudging over to the hamster. "I tried to be the best Hamster Helper I could be. But so far, I left your cage in Super Fluffy's reach and shrunk myself. Not only that, but I'm no match for your wiggle power. I can't hold you long enough to fly us both to the Ultra Grower!"

Frustrated, Ellie sat down and slumped against the blueprint. The paper unrolled across the desk, revealing a drawing of an aeroplane. It had aerodynamic angles that went this way and that.

Ellie's parents always studied drawings of normal objects, like boats or toasters. It gave them ideas for objects that were not so normal, like the Ultra Float or the Ultra Popper.

This drawing gave Ellie an idea too. It reminded her of Dex's paper plane.

If I had an aeroplane, I could fly us to the work table, she thought. *Wait a minute! That's not a bad idea . . .*

Ellie got straight to work. She flew one side of the paper over to the other side, folding the blueprint. Then she stomped along the fold to crease it with her feet. All the while, she kept Squeak in her super sight. The lab's rocket launcher was nearby. If he got too close, he could launch himself into orbit and become the first hamster in space.

After a few more folds and stomps, her paper plane was complete. Ellie stepped back and admired the aircraft.

"Well, look at that. Something good has come out of Dex's evil-doing," she said to herself. "Maybe that villain isn't so bad."

CHAPTER 8

Mad scientist

"All aboard the Ultra Plane!" Ellie sang. She flew Squeak over the giant paper wing and seated him snugly in the centre fold. Then she ran to the back and prepared to push off.

Grabbing hold of the tail, she started the countdown. "Three, two, one . . . GO!"

Ellie's heels kicked up dust as she roared like a racing car across the desk. Science journals and a microscope blurred past.

When the plane had picked up enough speed, she jumped on behind Squeak before they went soaring into the air. The plane sailed along smoothly. It caught an updraft from a blowing fan and flew higher.

From her bird's-eye view, Ellie looked down and smiled. The lab seemed like an exciting place where ideas could grow and blossom, and she decided she would enjoy exploring it – if she could grow herself first.

Soon, the work table came into view. Ellie turned to her hamster co-pilot. "Look, Squeak! We're getting closer to the Ultra Grower!" It lay beyond the island where most of the lab's formulas were stored.

As the plane glided down, Ellie pulled on the wings, steering over rows of colourful creations. They passed formulas that could change your shape and others that could change your species.

Straight ahead, a new formula was brewing in a large pot. *I better steer clear of that,* she thought. For all she knew, it would make them grow tiger stripes.

She carefully manoeuvred through clouds of steam. They were almost across the bubbling liquid when a huge bubble shot up behind them. It exploded with terrific force and threw the plane forward.

The paper aircraft was thrown over boxes of safety goggles. It headed towards an Ultra Safety Suit, which was hanging up on a rack.

"Prepare to land!" Ellie cried.

She flew off with Squeak and dropped into the suit. *Fwump!* They landed in a big, squishy pocket.

"Whew! That was a soft landing," she said. "I'm glad the Ultra Safety Suit is made with extra padding."

Just then, Mum's voice came from outside. "The brand-new Ultra Shrinker is finally complete. It's testing time!"

Ellie turned away from Squeak and peeked out of the pocket. Mum was walking towards them. Ellie was about to call out when Mum grabbed the Ultra Safety Suit off the hook. The sudden jerk sent Ellie flying back into the pocket.

Mum slid her legs and arms into the holes. She zipped up the suit as Ellie got to her feet, closing her inside.

Ellie sank back down. "Mum is going to test the new Ultra Shrinker. Until she's finished, we're stuck in this giant marshmallow. OK? Squeak . . . ?" She glanced over, but the hamster had gone.

Where did he go? Ellie wondered. Was it possible Squeak had crawled out when she wasn't looking?

Quickly, Ellie turned on her X-ray beams and peered through the suit, checking the lab outside. She could see the testing station where Mum had set up the Ultra Shrinker. Dad was watching from the other side of the glass doors.

Hmm. No hamster sightings anywhere, she thought.

While Ellie kept her eyes peeled, Mum plucked an apple off her desk. She put it on the Ultra Shrinker's platform, then stepped back and waited for the gadget to flash. But nothing happened. She waited longer. Still, nothing.

"I wonder why the new shrinker isn't working," Mum said to herself. She picked up the gadget to examine it, when strangely, she began to giggle.

More giggles followed. Suddenly Mum erupted into laughter.

"Whaaat's happening to Muuum?" Ellie cried, bouncing around the pocket with every hoot. It sounded like the failed test had made her cross. Not Ellie-didn't-tidy-her-room cross. But really brain bonkers!

Dad gave Mum a funny look. He must've thought her behaviour was odd too. "Is everything OK in there?" he asked.

"Something is loose in my suit!" Mum cried, doubled over from laughing. "It's moving around and tickling me!"

She pulled the suit off, and Squeak dropped out of the bottom. Ellie flew out of the pocket and scrambled after him as he ran behind the desk.

"Stop right there, Tickle Monster," Ellie said. She scooped him up and followed Mum out of the room. Squeak started wiggling again, but Ellie hung on as tightly as she could. She landed on the floor - she needed to catch her breath - as the door closed behind them.

While Dad brought the Ultra Shrinker to the work table, Mum checked inside the Ultra Safety Suit. She shook her head and hung it back up, then turned to Dad.

"I'm not sure what's wrong with the shrinker," she told him. "But it's nothing to laugh about, that's for sure. The gadget is almost due, and we're running out of time."

"I don't understand," Dad replied. "I put all one hundred and eleven microchips in the shrinker. At least, my calculations say so . . ." He motioned to some scribbled-out numbers on the whiteboard.

Suddenly, Squeak wiggled away from Ellie. He ran under the work table and stopped at a microchip that was lying next to Dad's stool.

Ellie caught up with the hamster as he poked his whiskers at the square chip.

"Dad needs to put this microchip in the new Ultra Shrinker," she said. "It must've fallen off the table when he was putting in the rest. No wonder the new shrinker doesn't work!"

Just then, Dad reached over his stool and picked up the Ultra Grower. He placed it beside the Ultra Shrinker.

"These gadgets are made the same way, but the Ultra Grower is operating just fine," he said to Mum. "Maybe if we take apart the grower, we can find out how to make the new shrinker work."

Mum clapped excitedly. "Brilliant idea!"

Ellie watched in disbelief as her parents opened their toolboxes. "Mum and Dad can't take apart the grower," she said. "What if it doesn't work when they put it back together? I could be stuck as a hamster-sized hero forever!"

CHAPTER 9

Shadow puppet show

Ellie's little life flashed before her eyes: Toaster
crumbs for breakfast. Baths in the sink. And school?
That was the worst part. She could already hear
the no-good names Dex would call her. Shorty the
Mighty. Super Squirt. The Incredible Shrimp.

*If I'm going to save the Ultra Grower, I need to stop
Mum and Dad,* she thought.

But how could she leave Squeak behind? The hamster could run off again. If only the lab had something that would keep him busy.

Ellie hopefully scanned the room when her gaze fell on the storage cupboard. Bulging out was a red, ripe and enormously round object. It was the supersized cherry!

She flew to the 60-centimetre-tall fruit. "Look, Squeak! It's your favourite treat!" she called.

The hamster perked up and scurried over. In no time, he started nibbling. Nothing was going to pull him away from the cherry, not even a monster tractor.

Without a second to lose, Ellie took off for the work table. There, her parents were taking out their tools, ready to turn the grower into a pile of mechanical bits.

Mum plucked a roll of measuring tape from the toolbox. Her hand shot to one side as she pulled out the tape to unwind it.

"Eep!" Ellie peeped, quickly ducking Mum's hand.

Circling around to a safer spot, she flew under the table and popped up behind Dad, who had just finished putting some screwdrivers in a row.

Pushing back his sleeves, he accidentally knocked Ellie with his elbow.

The bump sent Ellie flying backwards.

"Ouch!" She rubbed her bottom after hitting the ground hard. "Dad doesn't know his own strength."

Flying close to Mum and Dad seemed too risky. They were giants compared to Ellie, and one false move could be dangerous.

There has to be a different way to make them notice me, Ellie thought. *But how?*

It would take a big problem, even bigger than a broken gadget, to get their attention.

Just then Dad picked up a screwdriver and walked over to a tall lamp. He turned it on and tilted it towards the table.

His shadow crept over the wall as he passed the lamp to return to the grower. It reminded Ellie of Squeak's shadow puppets. She had thought they were made by the evil Shadow Puppet Master.

"A super-villain can get Mum and Dad's attention," she realized. "There's no bigger problem than that!"

As Dad went to loosen the first screw, Ellie bolted to the lamp. She stood squarely in front of the light and began making shadow puppet after shadow puppet.

She twirled into a figure skater. She flapped her arms like an eagle. She snapped a toothpick in half and boogied-down like a disco-dancing walrus.

"C'mon, Mum and Dad! Forget about the Ultra Grower!" Ellie shouted while swinging her toothpick tusks to a funky beat.

Next, Ellie moved like a mummy, moaning for effect. Then she turned into an acrobat, a moose and a kooky-spooky ghost. Shadows flashed on the wall as she feverishly changed from one thing to another. It was a show that would make even the Shadow Puppet Master stop and stare.

Finally, Mum noticed the shadows and looked up. She pointed hastily at the puppets. "Uh-oh! Trouble in the lab!"

Dad laid down the screwdriver. "The Shadow Puppet Master must want the Ultra Grower! Well, I'll stop his minions. All I need to do is turn off the light, and the shadows will disappear!" He moved the grower to the floor, then hurried to the lamp.

"Now's my chance!" Ellie flew to the grower. Flexing her mini muscles, she stood the gadget onto its side. It now towered over her like a giant hamster wheel. "I better roll this away from the work table," she said. "If the Ultra Grower flashes on Mum and Dad's tools, it will make everything bigger - not just me!"

She climbed inside and pushed the gadget forward. Just then, her mum gasped.

Mum was staring at the Ultra Grower. "The grower is moving away. A shadow puppet must have it!" She lunged for the gadget as Dad came running.

The Ultra Grower spun like Squeak's wheel as Ellie ran faster and faster. She could hear her parents' footsteps pounding the ground behind her.

Ellie kicked up her pedal power, gaining speed, and the grower charged across the lab. It raced under a bench and popped out into an open clearing.

"It's just the space I need!" Ellie dug her heels in hard, and the gadget skidded to a stop. She grabbed hold of the top and pulled the Ultra

Grower upright. It wobbled around before settling onto the floor.

Ellie glanced back at her parents, who were hurrying around the bench. Her heart thumping, she leaped onto the platform.

Suddenly, the Ultra Grower flashed.

Bit-by-bit, she started getting taller. Her legs and arms grew longer. Her body grew bigger. She slowly stretched up and out like her Elasticband Dude action figure.

* * *

Before long, Ellie was her full-grown super self.

She smiled at her reflection in the fridge door. "Phew! Now I won't have to pack crumb sandwiches for lunch."

"Ellie?" Mum and Dad froze on the spot, and their mouths dropped open. They quietly glanced from their daughter to the Ultra Grower.

Ellie handed the gadget to Mum. "I'm sorry I took the Ultra Grower," she said, breaking the silence. "I had to make myself big again. That is, after I got shrunk . . ."

"Shrunk?" Mum double-blinked. "But the last time I saw you, you were approximately 129-centimetres tall. You were upstairs taking care of Squeak."

"Squeak, squeak!" The hamster was still enjoying his biggest treat ever.

Ellie flew to the cherry and picked him up carefully. "Squeak got out of his cage," she explained to her parents. "Super Fluffy chased him into the lab. I ran after them and stepped on the old Ultra Shrinker."

"It worked that time, huh?" Dad asked.

Ellie nodded. "Looking after Squeak was really hard. I had to save him from noisy gadgets,

a hungry iguana and an exploding formula. I even had to save him from a mad scientist in a marshmallow suit!"

"It must've been hard work, indeed. But I'm glad it's finished," Mum said. She turned to the new Ultra Shrinker. "Unfortunately, I can't say the same for our work."

Just then, Ellie's brainpower sparked. She remembered finding the microchip that belonged in the gadget.

"Wait!" she exclaimed. "I know why the Ultra Shrinker isn't working!" Racing to the table, Ellie plucked the small square off the floor. She swung around and showed her parents proudly. "It's missing a microchip. *That's* why!"

"It looks like my calculations were incorrect," Dad said. He sat down with the shrinker and, after a few twists and turns, placed the microchip inside.

Then he put the cherry on the new-and-improved Ultra Shrinker to run one more test.

Everyone watched as the shrinker flashed. Everyone cheered as the fruit began shrinking.

"EUREKA!" Dad shouted when the cherry had shrunk down to its original size.

"Finally. Everything is ready for B.R.A.I.N.," Mum said. She smiled at Ellie. "You came to the rescue again. But I've been wondering something. Who let Squeak out of his cage?" She put up a finger. "Hold on! Let me guess . . . it was Destructo Dog."

CHAPTER 10

A mighty job

On Monday, Ellie ate breakfast with Squeak. She wanted to spend as much time with him as she could. Her job as Hamster Helper was almost finished, and she had to take him back to school soon.

Dad scooped more porridge into her bowl, then glanced at the clock. "Better eat up. You don't want to be late," he told her. He peeked at the hamster, who was nibbling his food in the cage. "You too, Squeak."

"Looking after Squeak was a big job, especially when I was 8-centimetres tall," Ellie said between spoonfuls. "Still, I'll miss having him around."

Mum put the bag of hamster supplies on the table. "He was a well-behaved guest," she said, packing up the rest of Squeak's food. "Except when he turned into a tickle monster."

Suddenly Super Fluffy ran into the kitchen with his ball. He stopped below the cage and whined for Squeak to play.

"Fluffster will probably miss Squeak the most," Ellie said. She bent over and patted her pup's head. "I know you want your new friend to come out again. But I'm not sure Squeak is ready for another game of chase with a giant drooling hairball."

She paused, her eyes widening. "Neither is this pet sitter!"

* * *

Mum and Dad drove Ellie and Squeak to school, then they had to deliver the Ultra Grower and Ultra Shrinker to B.R.A.I.N. Before they left, they offered to bring the supplies inside. But Ellie's super strength could handle everything without a problem.

She floated towards the main entrance when a paper aeroplane whizzed past. It turned sharply on a breeze and nose-dived at her feet.

Dex slunk out from behind a bush. "Curses, foiled again!" he said, clenching his fists. "I keep missing my target." He trudged over and picked up his weapon of major annoyance.

"Try folding your plane a different way," Ellie told him. "Maybe you should make the wings wider? In my experience, it helps the plane fly over updrafts . . . and bubbling science experiments."

Dex stared blankly. Then, he pulled a face and stomped away.

Flying into the classroom, Ellie placed the cage back on the shelf. Inside, Squeak was curled up in his hamster hut, sleeping.

"My duties are officially complete," she said to herself. "If only I had been more careful. Then I wouldn't have got into so much trouble . . ."

"Ellie!" Hannah came bouncing over. She was holding up a Dance Cat Academy sticker. "Look what I got on Dance Day at Winkopolis Books & Toys! I'm going to add it to my scrapbook."

"Cool!" Ellie said. She noticed Fifi, Ginger and the rest of the characters were on the sticker. "Hey, that reminds me! How was the trivia game? Did you win the poster?"

Hannah shook her head. "I got the last question wrong. I should've guessed the answer was KitKat! Anyway, I came in second place and won this . . ." She reached into her pocket and pulled out a KitKat charm bracelet. "I know you like Princess Power, but I want you to have the bracelet. That way we can match beacuse they already have one!"

"Wow, thanks!" Ellie said, slipping it on.

As the friends jingled their bracelets together, Miss Little walked up. "Hello, girls!" she greeted them. She turned to Ellie. "How is my Hamster Helper? I hope everything was OK this weekend."

"Well . . ." Ellie grew worried as she handed over the supplies bag. It was the same feeling that struck before she took Squeak home. She wasn't sure that she did do a good job. Hamster sitting hadn't gone very smoothly.

"I worked really hard at taking care of Squeak," she said. "I followed your instructions and even asked

Hannah for help with changing his bedding. But I still made mistakes."

"I'm sure they weren't too big," her teacher offered kindly.

"One mistake was small," Ellie replied, recalling the power of the Ultra Shrinker. "But the other one was huge. Squeak escaped after I left his cage on the floor. It was my fault." She shrugged a little. "I tried doing my best. But it wasn't good enough."

"Sometimes we make mistakes, even when we're trying our hardest to avoid them," Miss Little said. "What's important is you gave your best effort. Because you tried your best, you did a great job."

Suddenly a rustling noise came from inside the cage. Squeak had woken up and crawled out of his hamster hut.

He scurried to his door, where Ellie was standing. "Squeak, squeak!" he said.

"It sounds like Squeak wants to tell you something." Miss Little put her ear close to the cage and pretended to listen. "Aha! He says you did brilliantly too."

Ellie looked in and smiled at Squeak. She had made some mistakes while looking after him. But, no matter what trouble she'd faced, she had always tried to do her best. Because of that, she had done a great job after all.

GLOSSARY

aerodynamic qualities of an object that affect how easily it is able to move through the air

android robot that looks like a person

evil-doers people who do evil

formulas general facts or rules expressed in symbols, especially mathematical symbols

gladioli type of African plant related to irises with sword-shaped leaves and stalks of brilliantly coloured flowers

headquarters place from which a commander exercises command or the governing and directing centre of an organization

magnifier something that enlarges an object in fact or in appearance

nocturnal active at night

omnivore animal or person that eats food of both plant and animal origin

TALK ABOUT ELLIE!

1. As Hamster Helper, Ellie has many responsibilities. One of her jobs is to let Squeak exercise during the school day. Talk about why exercise is important for a class pet like Squeak.

2. Miss Little tries to calm Ellie's nerves about watching Squeak. What does she tell Ellie to make her feel better? Now, pretend you are Ellie's teacher. What would you say to help shrink her worries?

3. Ellie takes good care of Squeak. She gives him fresh water and keeps his cage clean. She even rescues him from the Ultra Hush-a-Bye! Look through the story and give two other examples of how she takes care of him.

EXPRESS YOURSELF!

1. Ellie wants to make sure she changes Squeak's bedding correctly, so she invites Hannah over to help. Write a paragraph about a time when you asked someone for help with a job. What was the job and who did you ask to help you?

2. Squeak's cage includes a food bowl, hamster wheel and other items. These things keep him happy and healthy. Imagine you are getting a hamster. Do some research and find out what belongs in a hamster's cage. Then make a list of the items that are needed for your pet.

3. Even though Ellie tries her best at hamster sitting, she still makes mistakes. Write a paragraph about why it's OK to make a mistake when doing something new. How can a mistake help you learn and do your job better?

ABOUT THE AUTHOR

Gina Bellisario is an ordinary grown-up who can do many extraordinary things. She can make things disappear, such as a cheeseburger or a grass stain. She can create a masterpiece out of glitter glue and shoelaces. She can even thwart a messy room with her super cleaning power! Gina lives in Illinois, USA, not too far from Winkopolis, with her husband and their super kids.

ABOUT THE ILLUSTRATOR

Jessika von Innerebner loves creating - especially when it inspires and empowers others to make the world a better place. She landed her first illustration job at the age of seventeen and hasn't looked back since. Jess is an illustrator who loves humour and heart and has coloured her way through projects with Disney.com, Nickelodeon, Fisher-Price and Atomic Cartoons, to name a few. In her spare moments, Jess can be found long-boarding, yoga-ing, dancing, adventuring to distant lands and laughing with friends. She currently lives in sunny Kelowna, Canada.

CHECK OUT THE REST OF ELLIE'S EXTRAORDINARY ADVENTURES!

ELLie ULTRA

Superhero for
School Council

by Gina Bellisario
illustrated by Jessika von Innerebner

ELLie ULTRA

Mighty Pet Sitter

by Gina Bellisario
illustrated by Jessika von Innerebner

ELLie ULTRA

Gina
Bellisario

An
Extra-Ordinary
Girl

ELLie ULTRA

Queen
of the
Spelling Bee

Gina
Bellisario

ELLie ULTRA

Gina
Bellisario

Super Fluffy
to the
Rescue

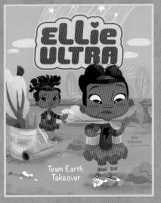

ELLie ULTRA

Gina
Bellisario

Team Earth
Takeover

THE FUN DOESN'T STOP HERE!

Discover more at *www.capstonekids.com*

Videos and Contests
Games and Puzzles
Friends and Favourites
Authors and Illustrators